When everyone was seated, the musicians began to play "America the Beautiful." Daisy almost had to pinch herself to be sure it was all real and that she and her family from St. Paul—originally from Liberty—Minnesota, were sitting next to the president of the United States at the White House! The sun shone, the garden sparkled from last night's rain, the taste of sweet punch was on her lips, and the music sounded heavenly. Daisy could not remember being so happy and excited. Things were going very smoothly.

Then everyone stood up for "God Bless America" and Aunt Ivy turned her ankle in her new shoes and pitched forward into her bowl of cream-of-watercress soup.

LOTTERY LUCK

NEXT STOP, THE WHITE HOUSE!

#6

Judy Delton
Illustrated by S. D. Schindler

Hyperion Paperbacks for Children
New York

For Poppy Balian Manthey—
who arranged the White House visit
—J. D.

First Hyperion Paperback edition 1995

A Hyperion Paperback original.

Printed in the United States of America.

1 3 5 7 9 10 8 6 4 2

Library of Congress Cataloging-in-Publication Data

Delton, Judy
Next stop, the White House! / Judy Delton ; illustrated by S.D.
Schindler—1st Hyperion Paperback ed.
p.   cm. — (Lottery luck ; #6)
Summary: When the Green family travels to Washington, D.C., to
place some of Mr. Green's sculptures in the White House garden,
irrepressible Aunt Ivy decides to use the opportunity to ferret out
corruption in the government.
ISBN 0-7868-1023-8
[1. Washington (D.C.)—Fiction.   2. Family life—Fiction.
3. Aunts—Fiction.]   I. Title.   II. Series: Schindler, S. D.
Lottery luck ; #6.
PZ7.D388Nen   1995
[Fic]—dc20   95-11602

CHAPTER 1

"I wish we could win the lottery all over again," said Lois to her best friend, Daisy Green. Daisy wanted to point out that *her* mother had won, not "we." Lois wasn't exactly a member of the family, though she did seem like one.

The girls were sitting on the front steps of Lois's new house in Minneapolis. The autumn sun was warm on their hair and shoulders. But it was low in the sky, and the days were getting shorter. The girls were a little bored, having had such an exciting summer. Now school had begun, and even though each of them was attending a new school, things had become routine.

Daisy was waiting for her aunt Ivy to come and pick her up and take her to the Greens' new home in St. Paul.

"I think we should get your aunt Ivy to buy us another ticket!" said Lois.

"We don't need any more money," said Daisy. "Anyway, we wouldn't be that lucky twice. I mean, you *knew* we would win last time. You don't have that feeling again, do you?"

Daisy looked at her friend to see if she had her psychic look on her face. The look that meant she knew what was going to happen next. (She didn't.) It happened to Lois quite often, though. Lois had known that their ticket, number 45707, would win.

Lois knew the Greens would sell their house in Liberty. And Lois even knew they were going on a cruise together before Daisy's dad told them!

There was no doubt about it, Lois knew a lot. Sometimes she knew more than Daisy's parents. (And she *always* knew more than Aunt Ivy!) Daisy listened to Lois. If it had not been for her friend, Daisy's mother would not have won the lottery, and winning the lottery changed the Greens' lives. They had gone to New York, been on the *Oriole Humphrey Show*, solved a hotel mystery, sold their condo, moved to a big house with a hobby farm in St. Paul, and gone on a cruise, all in the three months during the summer.

They had to move or else Artie, Gladys, Roxanne, and Olivia would have had to leave. The guests had seen the Greens on TV, come to visit, and never left. And the Greens had grown to love them, but there had not been room for ten people, plus all of Daisy's dad's metal garden sculptures in the Greens' little condo.

In their new house there was plenty of room for all of them. Lois's family had also left Liberty. They moved to Minneapolis, where her father had a new job.

"No, I don't see the winning ticket this time," she said, frowning and squinting and trying to feel psychic.

"We have enough money anyway," said Daisy. "It was just fun winning."

"You don't even need the lottery money anymore," said Lois. "Your dad is getting famous. My dad saw some of his sculptures in Washington, D.C.!"

"He does have a lot of new orders," said Daisy. "Since people saw us on TV."

Lois rubbed her forehead and got her trance-like look on her face.

"What is it?" said Daisy.

"I just had this idea," said her friend. "I mean, I know it's silly, but what if the president wanted to buy one of your dad's sculptures? I mean, they are in Washington. And that's where the president lives."

"The president doesn't go shopping in garden stores," said Daisy. "He's too busy running the country and stuff."

Lois closed her eyes. "I see him in the White House," she said slowly. "He's sitting at his desk in the Oval Office, looking at garden catalogs. He sees your dad's giraffe! He puts a circle around it! Now he's calling his wife in to see it. She's got flour on her hands because she's baking cookies for one of those parties they have. He asks her if she likes it. She says yes. She asks him if they can afford it. He says he has lots of money. . . ."

"This time you're way off," laughed Daisy. "No president reads garden catalogs. They plan trips to China and raise taxes and talk about criminals and doctors and stuff, not giraffes! And his wife doesn't bake, they have a cook."

Lois opened her eyes. "I suppose you're right," she said. "That would only happen in a movie."

But their life *was* like a movie, thought Daisy. Since winning the lottery, it seemed as if anything could happen. It was hard to believe Lois was wrong. But she had to admit, Lois's idea about the president was pretty far-fetched.

"My mom says I have a wild imagination," said Daisy. "But yours is worse."

"Here comes your aunt," said Lois. "I hear the police car."

Daisy's aunt Ivy was a meter maid, working in a division of the police department in St. Paul. It was Aunt Ivy's dream to be a private detective, and she liked to hang around with police officers and pick up tips. She was even going to night school and taking a correspondence course in detective work.

The police radio was spitting out static as she drove up and opened the car door.

"Guess what?" she said to the girls. "I have big news! We're going to Washington, D.C.!"

CHAPTER 2

Lois's mouth fell open. Daisy felt a shiver go down her back even though it was a warm day. Her friend's powers were getting scary. Maybe it was just a coincidence, a wild guess on Lois's part. Maybe they were just going to Washington on a vacation! That was it. That had to be it.

But they had just had a vacation! On a cruise ship! Why would her family go on another vacation?

As the police radio squawked, Aunt Ivy said, "The president wants to buy some of your dad's sculptures for the White House garden," she said. "Can you imagine that?"

The girls nodded their heads slowly. They could imagine that. They *had* imagined that.

So much for coincidence, thought Daisy. Lois's psychic powers had struck again.

"He saw us on TV on the *Oriole Humphrey Show*,"

Aunt Ivy went on. "The First Lady said, 'Let's get hold of that fellow and have him spruce up the garden.'"

Well, at least he didn't read catalogs like Lois had said. He watched talk shows on TV instead!

"A White House aide called your dad and ordered four big sculptures and said the president would like us to come to the White House for the installation ceremony. Lois, too. He wants to meet all of us who were on the TV show."

"Wow," said Lois.

"It's not a movie, it's real," said Daisy.

"Delphie's making a list of things he wants to tell the president. Like making the school day shorter and vacations longer. I thought I'd make a list, too. When will we have a chance like this again?"

At the rate their life was going, the chance was pretty great, thought Daisy.

Delphie was Daisy's younger brother. He was named after a flower, too, like everybody in the Green family. Even their dog's name was Larkspur.

"Get in," said Aunt Ivy, motioning to Daisy. "It's time to hit the road."

"I'll call you," said Daisy to Lois, "when I get all the details."

As they drove up to Winner's Roost, Delphie came dashing out of the front door, waving his notebook.

"We're going to sleep in the White House!" he yelled. "In that bed that George Washington slept in!"

Daisy's sweet mother, whose name was Iris, followed Delphie and said, "I'm sure we will sleep in a nice hotel in Washington, not in the White House."

"Unless the president takes a shine to you!" said Roxanne, who was from England.

"President!" said Olivia, Roxanne's little girl. *Fan* used to be her only word, but now she was repeating bigger words.

The family all trooped into the house, where Artie had made a special dinner of braised artichokes and leeks to celebrate the news. He liked to make healthy meals. Delphie wished Artie would make pork chops and mashed potatoes more often, but he rarely did.

Everyone talked at once, but then Daisy's dad explained the details.

"I talked to the president himself an hour ago," he said.

The family *oohed* and *aahed* at this news. The

president's own voice, right on their own telephone line! This was a historic moment, thought Daisy. And it happened at her own house, right in St. Paul, Minnesota!

"I told him I'd custom-make the sculptures, maybe something patriotic," said Mr. Green. "But he said no, he wants the animals he saw in the picture a senator had shown him: a bronze three-piece alligator and a water buffalo to put near the reflecting pool, and a unicorn and a rhino for among the roses. He would like them installed in time for the National Art-in-the-Garden celebration. I couldn't say no to the president, so I'll be busy this week putting the finishing touches on those sculptures."

The family was spellbound at this news. Finally, Aunt Ivy broke the silence, saying, "I thought I'd have to work because I just had time off for the cruise. But the boss said, 'Ivy, we can't be selfish about this. You have a chance to represent our state in D.C. and put in a good word for the Minnesota meter maids, and we want you to have that opportunity. You may even be able to slip in a word about more funding for new police vehicles. We'd welcome that.' So I shook his hand and thanked him and said I'd make the department proud."

"I can get time off, too!" said Delphie.

Mrs. Green got out the school calendar.

"There is a three-day holiday coming up in October for a teacher's meeting," she said. "That should work out just right."

"The ceremony will be on a Saturday, so we have a weekend, too," said Mr. Green looking at his calendar. "But it will take longer than that, because we have to drive. The animals can't be trusted to shippers; one small dent would ruin a rhino's tusk. I have to travel with them to make sure they are handled properly."

Did that mean the animals would ride in the car with them, wondered Daisy? Was she going to have to share a seat with not only Delphie and Aunt Ivy, but with a herd of pachyderms?

"I figured we would rent a van, drive out, and take a plane back," said Mr. Green. "The drive will take three days. And we want to do some sight-seeing."

It sounded to Daisy like even with the teacher's meeting and the weekend, they would have to miss some school!

"The children can miss some school," said Mrs. Green.

"It will be educational," said Gladys. "They

will learn more on the trip than they would in the classroom."

"I'll talk to your teachers," said their mother, "and see if you could write a report about Washington, D.C., to make up for the time you miss. Lois's mother can do the same thing."

Daisy frowned and Delphie whined, but it was worth a report to have time to spend in the capital, thought Daisy. And both she and Lois liked to write.

After dinner, Mrs. Green's friend Bunny burst in with her nephew Warren and an enormous cake. Warren had on a red, white, and blue shirt. The cake had red, white, and blue frosting and a flag in the middle. Bunny celebrated every occasion with a cake.

"What an honor!" Bunny exclaimed. "A little piece of Minnesota will be at the White House forever!"

Everyone had cake, even Olivia. When they left, Daisy and Delphie cleared the table, and Artie and Roxanne loaded the dishwasher. Gladys swept the kitchen floor. Afterward, Aunt Ivy motioned to Daisy to meet her in Daisy's bedroom.

"*Pssst!*" she said. "Follow me."

When they got to Daisy's room, Aunt Ivy said, "I don't want the others to know, but I consider this trip a great opportunity for me to serve my country. There is a lot of corruption in Washington, you know, and I feel called upon to use my special God-given talents as a detective to find the perpetrators. It's as if I was, well, chosen like Moses, to be a sort of missionary. A leader, if you will, among my people. I can't take this mission lightly."

Daisy sighed. She did not like knowing this. She did not want to be taken into Aunt Ivy's confidence. It was too much responsibility for her small shoulders. Besides, she was sure there were other qualified people who were doing that job already. Professional spies.

With Aunt Ivy spying on the government and her dad's animals riding in the car with them for two thousand miles, Daisy was not sure if Lois's prediction was something to rejoice over.

Not all predictions were necessarily happy ones.

CHAPTER 3

Even though the Greens had rented a van, six people and assorted metal animals would not leave much space for luggage. So Mrs. Green said, "We'll have to pare down. No extras this time."

"We can always tie stuff to the top," said Delphie. "We have to save room for souvenirs! I want to bring back White House T-shirts and stuff for Miles and me."

"Coming back we will be flying, so we can't buy too much out there," said Mrs. Green. "Of course we won't have the animals along then."

Daisy called Lois and told her to pack lightly. "The animals are the important thing on this trip, my dad says," said Daisy.

"No problem," said Lois. "My mom said I just have to take one good outfit along for the garden party. I mean, we can't wear jeans when we visit the president."

"I think the president wears jeans," said Daisy thoughtfully.

"I've never seen him wearing jeans on TV," said Lois. "He wears a suit and tie, and he has good haircuts."

"That's in public," said Daisy. "I'll bet when he digs in the garden and takes out the garbage and stuff, he wears jeans."

"The president does not take out the garbage!" said Lois, sounding shocked. "He has guys who take out garbage, it's their job!"

"Everyone takes out garbage sometimes," said Daisy, feeling cross with Lois.

Lois sighed. Daisy wondered if they were going to argue before they even left on this long drive.

"Well, who cares," said Lois. "The point is, no one will be wearing jeans at the garden party. Including us."

By the time they were ready to leave, everyone had agreed to pare down—except Aunt Ivy.

"I can't work without my new equipment," she said.

Her equipment was a new fingerprint kit, a camera with a large zoom lens that captured the action even if it was a block away, a sonar detector the police department had discarded when they got a new one, and a used microscope.

"For slides of blood samples," said Aunt Ivy. "As well as any evidence found at the scene."

Daisy shivered. "There won't be any blood samples," she said.

Daisy's mom was stern. "Ivy, we are going to a garden tea, not a manhunt. I am sure they have the FBI handy in case there is trouble."

Aunt Ivy shook her head. Then she sighed. "Civilians just don't understand," she said. "When you go through the bureaucracy, it slows things down. By the time the FBI is called in, the criminals could be in another state! I will be there undercover. This is my chance, Iris. My big chance! We will be right in the heart of what makes this country tick!"

"You can't take all that stuff, Ivy," said Mr. Green firmly. "You'll have to ship it."

But Aunt Ivy had no intention of shipping anything, Daisy was sure. When Aunt Ivy's bags were finally packed, they were bulging in strange places and were very unusual shapes.

As the day to leave for Washington grew closer, Mr. Green put the finishing touches on his sculptures. He polished them and buffed them till they shone like gold, even though they were just bronze. He padded them and wrapped them carefully so that they would be safe on the trip. And then he put them in the van.

"They should wear safety belts," said Delphie. "Like us."

"I think they'll be fine," said his dad. "We'll just keep our eye on them all the way so that they don't rattle or dent."

On the morning of departure, Artie hung a sign on the van that said WASHINGTON OR BUST!

Aunt Ivy stuffed a bulky bag in the back of the van when Mr. Green was not looking, and her handbag bulged at the seams.

Roxanne had made shortbread, which she packed in a plastic container. "I hope you have room for this," she said. "You'll be hungry on the road, and you can have it with a cup of tea from this thermos."

Gladys handed them a map she got from a friend who worked at the AAA.

"She's marked your route out for you, here in red marker," she said. "That is the best road to take all the way. But if you want the more scenic route, it's marked in green marker. That will take you longer, and the roads aren't as good."

Daisy was sure her father did not want to take the slow route with bad roads.

"Thank you all!" said Mrs. Green, giving them each a hug. "You take care of things, and we'll send you a postcard from the White House."

"We'll keep the home fires burning," said Artie.

"Burning!" shouted Olivia, waving bye-bye with both hands.

The family piled into the van, and Mrs. Green thought of last-minute reminders to call out as they left.

"Don't feed Larkspur too often. No table food! Don't let Olivia eat peanuts"—that was because babies choked on nuts—"and close the windows in case of rain. Leave a note for the milkman on Thursday."

"We'll do it all!" called Gladys. "Have a good time and say hello to the president for us!"

"Bunny didn't bring a cake," said Delphie. "She always brings a cake!"

Sure enough, as the van wound out of the driveway and onto the main road, Bunny came running down the street. In her arms was a big box.

"I'm so glad I didn't miss you!" she said. "This will taste good on the way! It's a marble cake."

The horn on top of the unicorn's head dug into Daisy's shoulder. Aunt Ivy was singing "From the Halls of Montezuma" off-key. And Lois was wearing some perfume that made Daisy sneeze.

"We're off!" said her father. "On the adventure of a lifetime! Think what memories we will bring home with us!"

Her father was right about that. There was no doubt about bringing memories home. But what kind of memories was another matter.

CHAPTER 4

"How long does it take to get to Washington?" asked Delphie, jumping up and down on the seat.

"It will take almost three days," said his father.

The family had been on the road for four hours. Aunt Ivy was taking a turn driving. Everyone but Daisy was munching on Roxanne's shortbread. Daisy felt a little vansick. She wasn't sure she ever wanted to see food again.

The van had just crossed the state line when the Greens heard a siren wailing. Flashing red lights appeared behind them.

"There must be a fire somewhere," murmured Mrs. Green.

"Or they are after a fleeing criminal," said Aunt Ivy.

Lois and Daisy turned around to look.

"They aren't going to a fire," said Lois. "Or chasing a criminal. They are chasing us."

"Aunt Ivy's speeding!" shouted Delphie.

Aunt Ivy glared at her nephew.

The police car pulled alongside the Greens and Aunt Ivy pulled over to the side of the freeway.

"I'll handle this," she said. "Just let me do the talking."

But the officer didn't want to talk. He came up to the window on the driver's side and asked Aunt Ivy for her driver's license.

This trip was not off to a good start, thought Daisy.

Delphie stopped bouncing.

Mrs. Green looked frightened.

"Is there a problem, Officer?" asked Mr. Green politely.

The officer looked to the rear of the van.

"It appeared that someone was trying to jump out of your rear window," he said. "But I see now, it isn't a person." He cleared his throat and frowned at the unicorn. "But there is an ordinance prohibiting objects from protruding from moving vehicles."

It was true. The unicorn that had been nudging Daisy now had its head out the window!

The officer wrote something on a clipboard he carried. Then he walked to the front of the car and wrote down the Greens' license plate number. When he came back to Aunt Ivy he said, "You seem to have an invalid driver's license, ma'am."

"Now just a minute, Officer," interrupted Aunt Ivy, leaning forward. "I am with the St. Paul Police Department, and I happen to know that I am not invalid."

"Your license has expired," said the policeman. "It was not renewed last month."

Aunt Ivy turned pale. "With all the excitement this past summer, I must have forgotten," she said.

"What is it you have back there?" asked the officer, nodding toward the back of the van.

"They are animal sculptures I am transporting to the White House, Officer," said Mr. Green. "The president called and requested them."

The officer gave a long low whistle. He tapped his pencil on the windshield of the van.

"Sure he did," he said slowly. "And my name is Elvis Presley."

"I can explain," said Aunt Ivy. "I didn't want to have to tell you this, but I am actually an undercover agent."

Aunt Ivy flashed her night-school certificate quickly and put it away again before he could read it.

"I'm going to do some work for the government in Washington," she went on, winking at the officer as if she and he were in on some little secret.

"You see, it's the perfect opportunity because we just won the lottery and the president saw us on TV and called and ordered these animals and summoned us to the capital, and when will I have another chance like this to investigate federal corruption?"

Now the officer's mouth was wide open. He stared at Aunt Ivy. Then he walked to his police car and got his police radio.

"Car fifty-nine," he said. "I need some backup. I've got a load of loonies here, with some possible loot that's missing from the museum."

"He doesn't believe us!" exclaimed Aunt Ivy. "He thinks we're lying! *And* he thinks we're thieves!"

"He thinks we're crazy!" said Lois.

"I can't imagine where he got that idea!" said Mrs. Green. "We are perfectly normal people."

Soon more sirens sounded, and two additional police cars, with more flashing red lights, came to a halt.

"You are going to be sorry for this," said Aunt

Ivy. "When your superiors find out about your mistake, you could lose your badge! You just call the president in Washington, and he'll set you straight! And he won't be pleased that you slowed us down. He is waiting for these animals for a garden tea!"

Now there were three officers standing with their mouths open. One shook his head back and forth. The other looked like he might laugh out loud any moment.

"I'm afraid we are going to have to search your van," said one officer.

"This is all a big mistake, Officer," said Mr. Green.

Delphie burst into tears and got out of the car with his hands up.

"Don't shoot!" he said. "I don't know these people! I didn't do it!"

"No one is going to shoot anyone," said one of the officers kindly. "We just have to investigate suspicious-looking vehicles. There's been a museum robbery, and, well, your story is, ah—a little suspicious. You have also violated two ordinances, numbers 839 and 458. Protruding object in moving vehicle, and driving without a valid license."

"Listen here!" said Lois, stamping her foot. "This family is a little strange, I admit, but they are not liars or thieves! These are Mr. Green's animals, and they are on the way to the White House and that's that!"

Daisy did not know whether to be flattered or insulted by Lois's words! She was glad Lois stood up for her family and defended them against lying and stealing. But did she have to say they were strange? Were they? Maybe Lois was right. Her family *was* odd. She'd have to live with that. Her dad had once told her that creative people were sometimes eccentric. But what was Aunt Ivy's excuse? She wasn't creative, but she was definitely odd.

While Lois was defending (or insulting) them, one of the officers was looking in the back of the van where the luggage was.

He whistled a long low whistle. "Hank," he said, to one of the other men. "Look what I found here!"

What could he have found? Animals were not illegal! Surely there were no drugs tucked away in their horns or tails.

The other two men went to the rear of the van. They unpacked Aunt Ivy's bulky bag. They took out the spy equipment and held it up.

"I thought I told you not to bring that!" cried Mr. Green.

Aunt Ivy looked embarrassed.

Now the police were sure they were on to something, thought Daisy!

"I'm sorry," said the first officer. "But we will have to take you in for questioning."

Now Delphie was crying loud and hard.

"I don't want to go to jail!" he cried. "I give up! I did it. I stole it! I'll give it back!"

Daisy was disgusted with her brother. Even he should know enough not to confess to something he didn't do.

"I'm sure this can all be cleared up quickly," said Mrs. Green. "My husband and sister are completely innocent."

"Follow us," said the first officer, getting into his squad car.

Mr. Green did as he was told.

Would the president get them out of this mess? thought Daisy. Would he fly out in *Air Force One* and defend their honor? Would he arrest the policemen and take the Greens into his private plane and help them escape? The president could do anything. No one had more power than he did. Not the king and queen of England. Not even TV stars.

But what if he didn't want to get involved? What if he wasn't home when her dad called him?

If this happened, then Delphie was right. Her sweet family was on their way to jail!

CHAPTER 5

"We are allowed one phone call," said Aunt Ivy, as they all trooped into the police station. "And I'm calling the White House."

On TV shows criminals called their *lawyers* with their one phone call. Were they on TV? Were they making a movie?

Daisy hoped Aunt Ivy would call her lawyer instead of the White House. But did she have a lawyer? Everyone in movies seemed to have one.

The Greens were led to a room with rows of chairs in it. Daisy was relieved it was not a cell. At least it didn't look like a cell. It had windows and a coffee machine. There were no bunks or bars.

"They're going to shine that light in our face till we confess," whimpered Delphie.

His mother soothed him and said, "We are perfectly innocent. There is nothing to worry about."

"Then why are we in jail?" wailed Delphie.

The Greens sat quietly on folding chairs. Even Aunt Ivy did not seem to have anything to say. After what seemed a long time, the officer in charge came back and said, "We are very sorry about your delay. We checked out your credentials, and everything seems to be in order. There was a museum heist in Ohio, and we have to check out all questionable behavior. But you will be free to go as soon as you pay the fine for the two violations."

"Aren't you going to fingerprint us?" asked Delphie, who seemed to be braver now that he found out that they could leave.

The officer shook his head. "You're clean as a whistle," he said, smiling. "You have an—er—interesting family, but not a criminal one."

Mr. Green paid the fines and took over the driving from Aunt Ivy, who was illegal the rest of the trip.

"Tell those animals out there to keep their heads in the car!" said one officer.

"We will, Officer," said Mrs. Green. "It won't happen again."

As they were leaving, one of the officers said, "You can tell me now, where are you *really* taking those animals?"

"To Washington," said Aunt Ivy. "To the president of the United States. Just as we told you the first time."

As the Greens drove away, the row of officers waved, and Daisy heard one of them say something that sounded like, "A nice family, but nuttier than a fruitcake. . . ."

"I'm glad we didn't have to call the president," said Mrs. Green. "It would be embarrassing to let him know we had broken the law."

"An ordinance isn't exactly a law," said Aunt Ivy. "Anyone can forget sometimes."

At the next state line, they got out to take pictures and have a picnic. Then Mrs. Green drove.

Mr. Green said, "I'll sit in the back and keep an eye on the menagerie. We don't want Uni here trying to get out again!"

Toward evening, the family stopped for dinner at a nice restaurant. Then they piled back into the car, and everyone—except Mrs. Green, who was driving—slept for a while. When it began to get dark, she drove to a hotel, where they spent the night.

"I hope Aunt Ivy doesn't cause any trouble tonight," said Lois, yawning.

"She won't," said Daisy. "She's too tired. We all are."

Daisy was right. The whole family slept like logs. The next morning they had breakfast and got back in the car for an early start. The sun was bright, and some of the leaves were beginning to turn to gold, as they drove east.

"I think we should reach Washington tomorrow," said Mr. Green. "If our driver doesn't wear out!"

But Mrs. Green liked to drive. The others played car games and counted how many different state license plates they saw. Then after lunch, Mr. Green read out loud to them from a book about sights to see in Washington.

"I like flying better than driving," yawned Delphie.

"You can't see as much," said Aunt Ivy. "Driving is educational."

"What's to see?" said Delphie. "Just a lot of cars and highways and trees and cows. I can see cows at home."

Everyone dozed off again, and soon Mrs. Green pulled over to a motel for the night.

The next morning they got another early start. Before too long, Mrs. Green called, "Look!"

Daisy rubbed her eyes and looked over where her mother was pointing.

"It's the Capitol building!" said her dad. "That's Capitol Hill!"

Aunt Ivy looked like she might cry. "The seat of our nation!" she said, dabbing her face with a tissue. "The land of the free and the home of the brave."

Mrs. Green stopped for a red light. Before they could stop her, Aunt Ivy jumped out of the car and kissed the grassy boulevard!

"She's crazy!" said Lois.

"She loves her country," said Mrs. Green. "Get back in the car this instant, Ivy!" she added impatiently.

" 'The land of youth and freedom, beyond the ocean bars. Where the air is full of sunlight, and the flag is full of stars,' " quoted Aunt Ivy, back in her seat. "That's Van Dyke."

Mrs. Green sighed and followed the street map of Washington, D.C. She drove toward the hotel where the White House aides had made their reservations.

"There's the Washington Monument Dad read about!" shouted Delphie. "I want to go up to the top of it!"

"There are the cherry trees," said their dad, pointing out the window. "If it was April they would be all in blossom. You'll never see cherry trees blossom in Minnesota!"

"Pennsylvania Avenue!" Lois read off a street sign. "That's the street the White House is on!"

"Does the president walk to work?" asked Delphie. "Or take a bus?"

"The president has a long black limo with a driver that takes him anywhere he wants to go," said Lois. "And besides, he lives in the White House. That's where he works."

All of a sudden, out of the blue Daisy saw the White House itself. There was a big fence around an enormous yard with a fountain, and behind it all was the big house with the white pillars.

The whole family stared at the White House.

"In a little while, we'll be inside, meeting the president," said Mr. Green.

Daisy couldn't believe it was all happening to her own family. They were really here! They would actually shake the hand of the president of the United States this very day!

After their unfortunate start, they had arrived safely. They would go home with lots of memories, Daisy was sure. But whether those memories would be happy ones, or catastrophic ones (given Aunt Ivy's propensity for trouble!), only time would tell!

But for now, their mother headed for the Grand Hotel.

CHAPTER 6

"So this little girl was responsible for the winning ticket!" said the president, a few hours later in the big hall in the White House. A limo had picked them up, and a nice woman had told them how to act in the White House—and now, here they were!

The president patted Lois on the head and shook her hand. "I saw you on TV and you are quite an actress!"

"Thank you, Mr. President," said Lois.

"And this must be little Pansy!" said the president, turning to Daisy and shaking her hand.

"My name is Daisy," said Daisy, turning pink. "Not Pansy."

She supposed the president had lots of names to remember; it was easy to make a mistake. On the other hand, the whole country trusted this man with their life and their tax money—was it too much to ask that he prepare a little better for guests? What if he was greeting a prince from Turkey and called him Prince Charles? What if he called Queen Elizabeth Queen Ann by mistake? This did not inspire confidence.

The president apologized, and Daisy turned a brighter pink. It was embarrassing to have to correct the president.

He threw back his head, opened his mouth, and laughed. He stood so close to Daisy that she could feel his warm breath and count his teeth. She could see his silver fillings. She was surprised the president *had* fillings. If he had to have his teeth filled, you'd think they'd be filled with gold, not silver.

He also had a little nick on his chin, Daisy could see, where he must have cut himself shaving that morning. Her dad did that sometimes, and he put a little piece of toilet paper on it till it stopped bleeding. She wondered if the president used toilet paper, or if his servants or Secret Service men had some special things just for presidents to use to stop blood flow.

The president moved on to Delphie and bent over to ask his name.

"Delphinium Green," said Delphie. "I'm named after a flower. We all are."

"How unusual!" said the president, giving Delphie a big smile.

Now Delphie stared at his teeth. Daisy was worried that he might say something unfortunate about school vacations. He did say something unfortunate, but not about school.

"You have a lot of teeth," said Delphie. "Do presidents have more teeth than regular people?"

Now the president really laughed. His shoulders shook, he laughed so hard.

But Delphie's parents were not laughing. In his lifetime, their son had one chance to meet the president, and of all the words in the dictionary to choose, those were not the most suitable. They tried to apologize for Delphie, but the president held up his hand and said, "Children are more truthful than adults." He laughed, "They always say what they think!"

Daisy hated to call the president of the United States a liar, but what he said wasn't exactly true. Daisy was a child, and she did not always say what she thought. If she thought something insulting, she did not say it. Period. Why was Delphie so obnoxious? Did he inherit some misplaced gene for manners? Maybe he was going to take after Aunt Ivy, who always said the wrong thing!

And besides, what did the president mean, children were more honest than adults? If that was the case, then adults should not be running the country! The president was an adult (supposedly), and if he wasn't as honest as children were, then a lot of people entrusted their country to the wrong man!

Now the president was asking Mr. Green about his sculptures and thanking him for coming to Washington with his family.

He asked Mrs. Green about gardening, and she told him about the roof garden she used to have on top of the condo in Liberty before they won the lottery and bought a house with plenty of room for a bigger garden.

"Liberty," the president mused, "what a fine name for a town!"

"Give me liberty or give me death," quoted Aunt Ivy.

"Yes, yes, indeed," he said, looking puzzled. "Patrick Henry, I believe."

Daisy thought that Patrick Henry had said, "I regret that I have but one life to lose for my country," but who was *she* to correct the president again? Anyway, maybe Patrick Henry said, "Don't shoot till you see the whites of their eyes." She frowned. How could she forget her history so fast?

Aunt Ivy grabbed the president's hand with both of hers and pumped it up and down.

"I can't believe I am touching our leader!" she cried. She kept pumping his hand, even though he tried to take it away.

"You must be Aunt Ivy," he said. "You are the one I heard the reporters referring to as Poison Ivy!"

Aunt Ivy looked aghast. "That was just a joke," she said. "I am really a very serious career woman you know. Dedicated to law and justice and order. I may use some of my skills at law and order right here in Washington. You know, you and I are sort of in the same business."

Lois rolled her eyes in disgust. "Your aunt is comparing her job to that of the president of the country!" she whispered to Daisy.

"Well I'm glad to have all the Greens aboard!" said the president. "Tomorrow we will see those fine sculptures and install them in the garden. I look forward to the party. I have work to do now, but the First Lady will show you the White House and join you for lunch."

The president shook their hands again and went off, followed by his Secret Service officers and his aides.

The president's wife stepped forward and shook their hands. She said lots of friendly words welcoming them to Washington. Then she led them on a tour of the White House.

As they walked, she told them that the house had more than 140 rooms.

"Wow," said Delphie. "I'd get lost trying to find the kitchen in time for supper!"

"This is the East Room," said the First Lady. "It is the biggest room in the White House. It is where we have all our parties and concerts."

"It looks bigger than a skating rink," whispered Daisy to Lois.

Next they went through the State Dining Room, where 140 people could eat, and to the Library, where 2,700 books were lined up on the shelves.

"I often come down here at night when I can't sleep," said the First Lady. "I sit and read till I get drowsy."

Daisy was surprised the First Lady could not sleep at night. Aunt Ivy said if you didn't sleep, there was something bothering your conscience.

Was the First Lady worried about something? Was she in some kind of trouble? Did her husband tell her bad news about the country?

Daisy didn't think it would be polite to ask her what kept her awake, and, anyway, they were climbing the steps now to see the Lincoln Bedroom.

When they got there, she pointed out furniture and paintings of interest. "These are all things from when Lincoln was president," she explained. "Some of them had been lost and have since been found and are back in place. This is his actual bed, and several other presidents have also slept in it. It was made extra long because Lincoln was such a tall man."

Daisy looked at the beautiful big carved bedstead. Her mother loved old furniture. Right now she was running her fingers over the silky wood. But not even all of the lottery money could buy Lincoln's bed. Some things even money could not buy.

Delphie looked like he would like to throw himself on the bed and jump up and down, and Daisy kept hold of the sleeve of his shirt.

Aunt Ivy was asking whether Abraham Lincoln carried a gun. When the president's wife said she did not think so, Aunt Ivy said, "Well he should have, you know. It may have saved his life at Ford's Theater."

Mr. Green was asking if the floors ever sagged in this old building (probably thinking of their Liberty condo), but their host said, "They used to sag; in fact; the place was falling apart in 1948. But Harry Truman moved out while they rebuilt the whole place on the inside with new metal beams. Now it is as sturdy as can be."

She sounded like she knew Harry personally, thought Daisy. "Harry moved out" and "Harry and I." But 1948 was a long time ago. Perhaps the beams would need to be replaced again, with so many people eating dinner and walking through the house on tours.

"There are thirty-two bathrooms in the house," the First Lady went on. "And in the kitchen, the cooks make food for about one hundred people a day."

"Does the president get much mail?" asked Delphie, thinking about his school report.

"We get about fifteen thousand letters a day," said the First Lady.

"I'll bet no one wants this postal route!" laughed Mr. Green.

The Greens also saw something called an "auto pen," which signed the president's name on letters with a real pen in his own handwriting.

"That's cheating!" said Delphie, entering it into his notebook.

The First Lady now stopped before a large painting of George Washington.

"We've got that picture on our wall at school!" said Lois.

"Well, this is the original of that one," said the president's wife. "And it has an interesting history. When the British troops set the White House on fire in the War of 1812, Dolley Madison would not leave until two men took the picture down so that it could be saved. Today, this picture that Dolley saved is the only thing that has been here since the White House first opened."

Now Daisy and Lois were writing in their notebooks along with Delphie.

"How do you spell 'Madison'?" asked Delphie. Lois told him.

The group started back down the stairs.

"Look," whispered Lois to Daisy, "all those people are in line to tour the White House." She pointed. The line wound outside and down the sidewalk.

"We're lucky to have our own private tour with the president's wife," Daisy said.

"And we are the only ones who get to eat in the White House!" said Delphie. "Hey," he said, remembering something. "I forgot to read my list to the president. Of what he needs to do."

"I forgot, too," said Aunt Ivy, "but there's plenty of time later."

"I don't think the president wants suggestions from us," said Mr. Green firmly.

"This is a democracy," said Aunt Ivy. "In a democracy the people make suggestions."

The First Lady was showing the Greens some new draperies in the State Dining Room when Daisy noticed that Delphie was missing.

"And now I'll leave you at the rest rooms here to freshen up before lunch," said the president's wife. "Mr. James will bring you along when you are finished."

Mr. James went into the men's rest room with Mr. Green. Daisy looked around for her brother.

"*Psst!*" said Delphie from behind a large statue. "Over here! Come see what I found!"

CHAPTER 7

"It's a key!" said Delphie, holding something up for the girls to see. "It might be the key to the front door of the White House! Or the key to the Capitol or the U.S. Treasury. Or that place they make the money."

"The Mint," said Lois. "You can't keep it. It's government property."

"Pooh," said Delphie. "I'm keeping it. There's no name on it. Finders keepers, losers weepers."

"Somebody lost it, and we have to turn it in," said Daisy, trying to get the key out of Delphie's hand. The children scuffled, and suddenly Daisy let go of Delphie's arm, and he flew backward and into a large green china urn. The urn wobbled and finally fell against the marble wall and cracked down the middle!

Lois and Daisy stood as if they were glued to

47

the spot. Their eyes grew large, and their mouths fell open.

Finally Daisy said, "You broke part of the White House! Delphie, you ruined part of the government!"

The three children looked at the urn.

"It isn't broken," said Delphie. "It's all in one piece."

"But it's cracked!" said Lois. "Right down the middle!"

"What do they do to people who crack the president's furniture?" asked Daisy.

"Maybe they send them to one of those Greek islands, like exiles. Or maybe to Siberia, where it's freezing cold," said Lois.

Delphie burst into tears for the second time since the trip started.

"Be quiet," said Daisy. "We don't want anyone to hear us! Besides, Siberia can't be any colder than Minnesota."

"I don't want to go to Siberia!" sobbed Delphie.

"Well they might make you go," said Lois. "They might just put you on one of those freighters that cross the ocean and don't come back."

Daisy shot Lois a frown. She was definitely making things worse.

"There's nothing to do but confess," said Lois. "Let's go tell the president's wife it was an accident."

"You made me do it!" cried Delphie. "You pushed me!" he said to his sister.

"Did not," said Daisy.

"Did, too," said Delphie. "Anyway, no one saw us. They don't know it was us."

Daisy looked up and down the hall. It was true. No one was in sight. But what did that matter? They had done it, and they knew they had done it!

"Why don't we just fix it ourselves?" asked Lois. "Maybe we can paint over the crack or something. Have you got any green paint?" she asked her friend.

"Do I look like I have green paint with me?" demanded Daisy.

"I know what we can do," said Delphie. "We can turn the side with the crack toward the wall!"

He ran over and put his arms around the urn. With Lois's and Daisy's help, they managed to turn the giant vase in a half circle till the crack was in the back. When they stepped back, there was no sign of the break.

The rest room door opened just then, and Aunt

Ivy and Mrs. Green came out. Then the other door opened, and Mr. James and Mr. Green came out, laughing and talking.

"Boy, that was just in time!" said Lois. "No one would even know that thing had a crack in it."

"It's no good for anything anyway," said Delphie. "It's too big to put a bunch of flowers in."

"It's probably a very valuable Chinese vase," said Lois. "From the Ming dynasty or something."

Where did her friend come up with these things? wondered Daisy.

"My uncle collects antiques," said Lois, reading her mind. "He's got a Ming vase that's worth about a million dollars."

A million dollars! If Delphie broke a million-dollar vase, her family would have to buy the president a new one! It was lucky they had won all that money in the lottery! At least that money might keep Delphie from sailing off on a freighter to Siberia!

Or maybe they'd have to replace it and be exiled! Daisy's mind was spinning. This was if they confessed, of course. And they would have to confess! The president himself had said children were honest. How would it look when the son of his favorite sculptor was found to be a liar? A big liar!

"Aren't you children going to wash up?" asked Mrs. Green. "We have to be joining the others for lunch soon."

The children went in to wash their hands.

"Look at the monogrammed towels!" whistled Lois. "Not even paper towels!"

Daisy could see that Lois was not going to lose time worrying about the broken vase. It was up to her, Daisy, to save the honor of her family and do all the confessing.

When the girls came out of the rest room, Aunt Ivy was leaning up against the green Ming vase, writing something in her notebook. All of a sudden, the vase gave way and swayed.

"Watch out!" cried Mrs. Green.

Mr. James ran to the rescue, and together he and Aunt Ivy grabbed the vase.

"Just in time," said Mr. Green. "That was close. You better be more careful, Ivy."

But as Mr. James straightened the vase, the large crack appeared!

"Oh, Ivy, look what you've done!" cried Mrs. Green. "You cracked the vase!"

Aunt Ivy turned white as a sheet. "But it didn't fall over!" she said. "How could it have cracked?"

"Those things are quite fragile," Lois told her. "Probably just one little bump like that did it."

"Don't worry," said Mr. James. "It was an accident. I don't know the value of the item, but I am sure it is fully insured."

Aunt Ivy had seemed ready to cry, but Mr. James's words seemed to cheer her. She looked like she might hug him. Delphie was skipping down the marble hall thinking about lunch and the key in his pocket, the urn forgotten.

Lois was talking with Mr. James about a painting over the fireplace.

It looked like it was Daisy who would carry this deep dark secret inside of her forever. Even though the vase might be insured, it was wrong to let Aunt Ivy think she had done it. But Delphie and Lois looked like they had already forgotten the whole incident.

If Daisy told Aunt Ivy, she would turn Delphie in, and her brother would hate Daisy forever. She wished that she was in that long line of people on tour outside, whom no one knew. No one in that line would break anything.

The president's wife was waiting for them,

smiling. She won't be smiling when she finds out poor Aunt Ivy broke a Ming vase, thought Daisy! She would probably tell her husband tonight when they were alone at dinner.

"Do you know what that silly woman detective from St. Paul did today?"

"Who, old Poison Ivy?" the president would ask.

"She broke our priceless Ming!"

"Off with her head!" the president would cry.

Daisy caught herself. They were not down a rabbit hole in *Alice in Wonderland*! No one chopped off your head for breaking a vase in real life! It was her wild imagination again. It always got her in trouble.

"Sit down, won't you?" said the president's wife.

Even though there were place cards, Aunt Ivy slipped into the chair next to Mr. James.

"Your Aunt Ivy likes that guy!" whispered Lois to Daisy. "I think she has a crush on him."

"That's silly," Daisy whispered back. "She's just grateful he told her the vase was insured."

But was it silly? It would be like her aunt to fall for someone in uniform. Even if it was just a White House–attendant uniform.

On the table, there were plates rimmed in gold and napkins with the White House seal on them. At each place was a crystal wineglass that sparkled in the sun. Delphie already had picked his up and was looking inside it.

Please, begged Daisy to herself, don't let Delphie or Aunt Ivy drop a wineglass and break it!

"Isn't that great that Aunt Ivy thought *she* broke the vase, instead of you?" said Lois when they were being served tiny salads with mint leaves around the edge.

Lois used an unfortunate choice of words. In the first place, it wasn't Daisy who broke the vase; it was Delphie. And in the second place, it wasn't "great" that Aunt Ivy thought she broke it.

"No," said Daisy. "I mean, it takes the blame off Delphie, but it's not fair. She didn't do it."

"Pooh," said Lois. "Aunt Ivy is always in trouble. She's like a walking bomb, ready to go off at any time."

What Lois said was true, but that didn't mean that every single thing that went wrong should be blamed on Aunt Ivy! Here she was innocent, for once, and getting blamed anyway! It was something like the boy who called "Wolf! Wolf!"

in the fairy tale. No one believed him when it was true. No one gave Aunt Ivy credit when she was innocent!

Should Daisy come clean and save her aunt? Should she turn in her little brother to save her aunt?

CHAPTER 8

That night Daisy did not sleep well, even though the hotel had thick comfortable mattresses and fluffy down pillows. Even though Aunt Ivy seemed to have forgotten about the accident, Daisy knew it was unfair to hold back evidence.

The other thing that worried her was the key Delphie had found. After the lunch at the White House, he had been sneaking down halls trying it in all the doors he came to.

"It doesn't fit any door around here," he had said. "I think it's the key to where they make the money. We could sneak in at night and help ourselves!"

Daisy was really alarmed now. It was not enough that Delphie broke the vase and didn't tell. Now he was planning a full-scale robbery! She could see her small brother's face splashed across the newspapers and on TV news.

CHILD ROBS MINT IN D.C.! it would say. GIVEN A LIFE
SENTENCE IN SING SING.

Where in the world was Sing Sing anyway?
Daisy wondered. And was it a place where the
prisoners were members of a chorus? Since
Delphie could not carry a tune, she hoped he
wouldn't be sent there.

Daisy shook her head briskly. She was acting as
if it really had happened. Chances are the key was
not to the Mint. And chances are when it came
right down to it, Delphie would not take anything, even a pencil, that did not belong to him.
Yet . . . how could she be sure?

The next morning it was raining. It was the day
of the garden party. A clap of thunder woke Daisy
up. She was relieved that even someone as pow-
erful as the president had no control over the
weather at his own important parties.

"The party isn't till one o'clock," said her dad.
"Mr. James suggested we take a tour of Washington this morning!"

"Good," said Aunt Ivy. She had been disap-
pointed to find no corruption within her reach at
the White House. Daisy was sure she wanted to
check the other government buildings.

"You know what this means," said Delphie to

Lois and Daisy. "It means I can try my key in doors everywhere we go!" He held it up and dangled it in front of their eyes.

"I think it will be a good time to take notes for our report," said Lois.

After breakfast, Mr. James came with big black umbrellas and shepherded them all into a black limo. Aunt Ivy kept up a running conversation with Mr. James and asked him a lot of questions.

The car took them to the Lincoln Memorial, where Mrs. Green got them all out in the rain to line up and have their picture taken.

At the Washington Monument, Delphie insisted on going inside and climbing to the top. "It's for my report," he said.

Everyone waited in the car while Delphie and Aunt Ivy went inside. Before very long, Aunt Ivy came out. When she got to the car, the family noticed she looked green. "I forgot that I'm afraid of heights," she said.

"Put your head between your knees," said Mr. James. "That sometimes helps when you are dizzy."

In ten minutes, Delphie came bouncing out of the monument with his notebook and said, "Aunt Ivy got sick!"

The limo moved on, and the family spent some

time in the National Archives and in the Air and Space Museum.

"It's too bad we don't have an entire day here," said Mr. Green. "There is just too much to see in Washington for such a short visit."

"Well, we are really here to install the animals," said his wife. "That is the most important thing this visit. Next time we will have to come just to sightsee."

The limo stopped again at the Smithsonian Institute, where Daisy and Lois wrote down quickly as much as they could of what they saw.

In all of the buildings, Aunt Ivy dusted for fingerprints while the guide kept the others' attention talking about historical documents, artifacts, and famous paintings.

Delphie was short enough to slip under raincoats and umbrellas and to thrust his key into any lock he saw.

It was during a slide show in the National Gallery, when all the lights were out, that Delphie and Aunt Ivy both disappeared. They were there when the lights went off, Daisy knew, but when they came on again, there was no sign of them.

"They're probably just in the bathroom," said Lois, with no interest.

Mr. and Mrs. Green were absorbed asking questions about the French modernists and did not notice their absence.

"I can't wait to show you the African sculptures!" said Mr. James, pleased to have two people with him—one of them a professional artist himself—who were so interested in art.

After the African exhibit, the Greens went on to a display of Egyptian shards. There was still no sign of Aunt Ivy and Delphie. Her parents were wearing earphones now, for a better description of the artwork. Daisy and Lois sat down on a stone bench beside a large potted palm.

"It's almost noon; what if we have to leave without them?" asked Daisy.

"Well, it's not like anyone would kidnap them or anything," said Lois. "I'm getting hungry."

"The key!" said Daisy. "It could be valuable! Maybe someone kidnapped Delphie to get the key!"

"And they probably kidnapped Aunt Ivy for being crazy!" laughed Lois.

They were both wrong. Just when they were ready to leave for the hotel to get ready for the party, there was a loud noise. A piercing siren went off over their heads, and iron gates sprang closed in front of all the exits.

The noise of the siren was deafening. And it did not stop its shrill blast.

"Is it an air raid?" shouted Mr. Green.

"Where is Ivy?" demanded Mrs. Green.

"It's just the security system," said Mr. James. "It's for emergencies, like robberies or fire. Sometimes it goes off by accident. It's a sensitive system."

Daisy and her mother both had the same nervous feeling in their stomach that this was not an accident. They both had the feeling that Aunt Ivy was at the bottom of this. It wasn't only Lois who had psychic abilities.

A group of guards gathered in the center hall. They were looking at a TV monitor above them. On the screen, Daisy could clearly see two people in a room alone. One was tall, and one was short. Outside the room, guards were trying to force the door open.

"I'll find out what has happened," said Mr. James.

But Mr. James could not get out of the Egyptian room. The guards and the gates kept everyone prisoner.

After what seemed like ages, the siren stopped and the gates sprang back, and a group of guards

led Aunt Ivy and Delphie into the room. Delphie ran up to his mother and threw his arms around her.

"We got locked in a storeroom! It wasn't our fault! We just opened a door and it closed behind us and we couldn't get out," he cried.

"I didn't see any warning on that door," said Aunt Ivy. "They should let people know when it's off-limits."

"It said PRIVATE. NO ADMISSION on the door," said the guard. "In red letters. When that door is opened, the siren sounds immediately for security purposes."

"All's well that ends well," said Mr. James. But he did not sound as forgiving this time of Aunt Ivy's faux pas as he had when she toppled the vase.

As the family got into the limo, Aunt Ivy said, "I know there is something in that room that needs to be investigated. Otherwise, why would everyone be forbidden to go into it? Why would it be off-limits to the taxpayers?"

Mrs. Green sighed. Mr. James looked cross. The Greens must not have been his easiest charges, Daisy thought.

"It was probably off-limits because they can't

have people wandering into storerooms breaking valuable things," said Mr. Green.

But Aunt Ivy did not look satisfied. "I say there's trouble in there," she said.

"My key almost fit in that lock," whispered Delphie to Daisy and Lois.

"Don't hang around with Aunt Ivy," Lois warned him. "It will just get you into trouble."

The family tumbled out of the limo at the hotel and ran up to their rooms to dress for the party.

"I'll pick you up in one hour," said Mr. James tersely. "Be sure you're ready."

"He was such a happy man yesterday," mused Mrs. Green. "He seems a little cross today."

I'd be cross, too, thought Daisy, if the president saddled me with the care of a family that broke the White House vases and set off sirens in the National Gallery. She hoped her family wouldn't cause the poor man any more trouble at the garden party. One thing she was sure of, he'd be happy and relieved when they got on the plane to return home!

CHAPTER 9

The Greens put on their party clothes, and so did Lois. When Aunt Ivy came out of her room wearing a pink lace floor-length dress, everyone stared. The dress seemed to have too much material and too many ruffles. It stuck out on all sides and swept the floor. With the dress, high heels, and a very curly hairdo, this woman did not look like Aunt Ivy! She wore dangling earrings and a sparkly necklace. All of Aunt Ivy glittered.

"I think she's dressed up for Mr. James," whispered Lois.

"It's her White House outfit," said Daisy defensively. "I think she bought it before she met Mr. James."

"Well?" said Aunt Ivy. "What do you think of my new dress? I just got it yesterday at the dress shop in the hotel. The shoes are new, too. The latest style, the woman told me."

Lois nudged Daisy. "See?" she said to her. "This dress is Mr. James–bait!"

"It's—er—very nice, Ivy," said her sister. "There seems to be a lot of it."

Mr. Green frowned. "Can you walk in those things, Ivy?" he said, looking at her shoes.

Aunt Ivy said yes, but when she walked, she tottered. Then she stumbled. She was not used to high heels after wearing those heavy, flat metermaid shoes that were regulation for the whole police department.

When Delphie saw Aunt Ivy, he looked puzzled. "Whose dress have you got on?" he asked.

Aunt Ivy ignored him.

"She looks like the tooth fairy!" said Delphie to his sister. "She just needs one of those sticks."

Daisy gave him a warning look. "You mean a wand," she told him.

The family was ready and waiting when the limo arrived. Mr. Green looked uncomfortable in his tuxedo, and he looked worried.

"I hope I don't have to say much," he said.

"I think the president will do the speaking," said his wife.

On the way to the White House, the sky cleared and the sun came out.

So the president *did* have party power after all, thought Daisy! The sun came out just in time for the garden ceremony. It would have been awful if the party was inside and her dad's sweet animals were outside, where no one could see them in their new home.

But when the Greens got out of the car and went through the house and veranda to the garden, the animals stood sparkling among the flowers and shrubs. They looked like they had lived there all their lives!

Tables with white linen tablecloths, set with pretty garden plates and sparkling silver and crystal, were placed on the green lawn. Colorful flowers and fruits, along with place cards, graced each table.

On the veranda overlooking the garden was a long table set up for the president, his wife, special guests, garden-committee members, and the Greens.

People poured into the garden, shook the president's hand, and were introduced to the Greens.

"And this is our hero, the sculptor," said the president, giving Mr. Green a pat on the back of his rented tuxedo. "He is responsible for the glory in the garden, which America will enjoy for years to come."

Daisy wondered how America would enjoy it, except in pictures. Most of America never got to the White House. It was the president who would enjoy it. And since he bought the animals with his own money instead of the taxpayers', Daisy wondered if he would take them along when he left office. It would be hard to find another garden where so many animals would look good, she thought.

Waiters came around with fancy drinks in glass flutes. There was pink punch (which matched Aunt Ivy's outfit) and little glasses with umbrellas in them for the children.

"Hey, look!" shouted Delphie. "They don't even use paper cups for picnics!"

The president laughed, and the others tittered politely. Daisy nudged Delphie and whispered, "This is not a picnic!" in his ear.

"It's outside," he shouted. "It is, too!"

Daisy was glad to notice some of the other women also had long dresses on. Not as ruffly and pink or as big as Aunt Ivy's, but they were fancy.

One by one, people came up to the Greens and

were introduced. They all said nice things about the garden animals, and many of them asked Mr. Green how he made them.

Aunt Ivy was tottering over toward Mr. James, but he seemed to be avoiding her.

"She's *chasing* him!" said Lois. "How embarrassing!"

Daisy wondered if somewhere in that dress there were pockets holding Aunt Ivy's equipment. It was not like her to be without her spy things.

A waiter with a white towel over his arm came up to the Greens with a tray of canapés. There were little round sandwiches, stuffed olives, and something red on a toothpick. Each of the Greens took one, except Delphie, who took six.

"Put some of those back!" said Daisy. "That's greedy! And it's impolite!"

"It's my lunch!" he said, putting them into his pocket. "I need more than one of those little things for lunch!"

"It's not lunch," said Lois. "It's appetizers. It's to make you hungry for the real lunch."

That was something Delphie did not need, thought Daisy. Something to make him even hungrier.

On the veranda a small group of musicians assembled. Soft music began to play.

"Aunt Ivy should be playing that thing," said Delphie, pointing.

"That thing is a harp," said Lois.

Delphie nodded, his mouth full of food. "It's the thing fairies play in heaven," he said. "I saw them in pictures."

Lois rolled her eyes in disgust. "Those are angels, not fairies," she said.

"Well, they look like Aunt Ivy," said Delphie.

Mr. James and the other aides were now directing people to the tables. Lunch was about to be served. The Greens and Lois waited until the president and his wife were seated and then sat down by their place cards.

When everyone was seated, the musicians began to play "America the Beautiful." Daisy almost had to pinch herself to be sure it was all real and that she and her family from St. Paul—originally from Liberty—Minnesota, were sitting next to the president of the United States at the White House! The sun shone, the garden sparkled from last night's rain, the taste of sweet punch was on her lips, and the music sounded heavenly. Daisy could not remember being so happy and

excited. Things were going very smoothly.

Then everyone stood up for "God Bless America" and Aunt Ivy turned her ankle in her new shoes and pitched forward into her bowl of cream-of-watercress soup.

CHAPTER 10

"Accidents do happen," said the First Lady after the song was over, as she mopped up the cream-of-watercress soup from Aunt Ivy's pink ruffles with a White House napkin.

"This isn't exactly the way to win Mr. James's heart!" chuckled Lois quietly.

Poor Aunt Ivy! How accident-prone could one person be?

The attendants tried to pretend nothing had happened, and the president asked questions about Minnesota, just as if no one had fallen into a bowl of soup at his table.

"That's real class," said Lois. "These people know how to handle social gaffes."

Daisy wondered what Lois meant by a social giraffe. And what did it have to do with falling into a bowl of soup?

The Greens got through the rest of the luncheon with no more social giraffes, and after the dessert (which left Delphie with a chocolate mustache), the president of the garden club gave a long talk about the new bulbs set in the lawn. Then there were more speeches, and finally someone announced the president. He got up and gave a short talk about how fortunate they were to have the sculptor of these lovely statues present today.

"It is an honor and a privilege to support artistic endeavors of individuals like Mr. Green," he said. "We are proud of the art in the White House, and now we are proud of our garden as well. There will be a permanent plaque on the lawn in your honor."

Then the president introduced Mr. Green, and he stood up and said it was an honor for the Greens to be there and that he was proud to be asked to contribute to such a historic cause.

Several members of the audience and the garden committee had questions. One woman asked if the animals would rust, and Mr. Green assured her that the rain, sunshine, and snow would only improve their appearance. "Exposure to the elements gives them a fine patina over the years," he said. "They will look good long after you and I have worn out," he said cheerfully.

The woman looked startled and then frowned. She did not like to think she would wear out before a metal alligator, Daisy imagined.

Before he sat down, Mr. Green announced that his family would like to make a donation to the garden club, "To support other artistic garden beautification and development projects."

He handed the chairperson of the garden club a large check, and there was thunderous applause.

"Why, that is very generous of you," said the president, applauding with the others. "I am sure it will be put to good use."

"We may be able to get that greenhouse we need so badly here!" said the woman who did not want to wear out before the alligator.

After all the talks were over, people sat down and drank coffee and tea and tiny after-dinner drinks that looked like small sundaes but weren't. If they had been ice cream, surely she and Delphie and Lois would have got one, too. Instead, they got more fruit punch.

Mrs. Green was talking animatedly to the First Lady about horticulture.

"I say chemical fertilizer is inferior to the real

thing," she said. "I stick to manure and ground fish stock for my garden."

The president's wife frowned over that controversy. She said she wasn't positive, but that she knew that the commercial fertilizer had worked well on the daffodils, and that manure smelled bad.

Daisy and Lois sat at the table and graded the dresses the women wore.

"Aunt Ivy's gets an F," said Lois.

"Well, it would be OK if it was a bridesmaid dress at a wedding," said Daisy thoughtfully.

Lois shook her head. "It's too ugly for a wedding."

Perhaps she was right, thought Daisy. There was no hope for the dress. Especially since it now had a green stain down the front of it from the watercress. Aunt Ivy should not shop alone.

Delphie was busy pretending his place card was a race car and was making *vrooming* noises around the bowls of flowers. None of the children were listening to the adult conversation. That is, not until the president's wife said quite loudly, "Well, we don't know how it happened. We just got up one morning, and it was broken. But the perpetrator will be punished," she said vehemently.

All of a sudden, both Aunt Ivy and Delphie stood up and said, "I did it!"

Everyone at the table stared at them. (For the second or third time.)

"I broke it!" said Delphie, who was trying hard not to cry.

"No, I did!" said Aunt Ivy, puzzled at why Delphie was confessing to her crime.

"And I found this key to the Treasury," said Delphie, taking it out of his pocket and putting it down on the table in plain sight. "Here, take it!" he said, sliding it forward.

The president's wife looked shocked. "You broke the hall window?" she said to Delphie and Aunt Ivy.

"Window?" said Delphie.

"Window?" said Aunt Ivy.

"You broke one of the White House windows?" echoed Mrs. Green.

Daisy was rejoicing that Delphie had come clean, while Delphie was realizing that he shouldn't have. It was not the vase they were talking about, but a window! That's what comes of eavesdropping, thought Daisy. If a person listens, they should listen to the whole story. Not just the end of it.

The matter was finally straightened out, and the president's wife said, "Mr. James told us about the vase. That's just an inexpensive reproduction. We can't have the real thing in the entry hall. Accidents do happen, you know."

She got up and gave Aunt Ivy and Delphie a hug. "You're not to worry about that. All's well that ends well, you know. Now do you have any idea who broke the window?"

Delphie and Aunt Ivy shook their head vigorously.

"I don't know anything about that," said Aunt Ivy.

"Neither do I," said Delphie.

"Time will tell," the First Lady said. "The truth will come out."

"This woman's full of original sayings," scoffed Lois.

Daisy did not think they should find fault with the First Lady. After all, she *was* kind and forgiving and didn't lock either Aunt Ivy or Delphie up in Sing Sing. That alone was worth something.

"And here is my little bureau key!" she exclaimed, pouncing on Delphie's key to the Treasury! "I wondered where that could have gone to!"

"I found it behind a statue," Delphie muttered.

"Well, thank you, dear!" she said.

"What's a bureau?" Delphie asked the girls.

Lois laughed. "It's not the U.S. Treasury!" she said. "It's the chest that the president and his wife keep their underwear in!"

Delphie looked disgusted. "That key was just to get to someone's underwear?" he asked.

"Well not just any underwear," said Daisy. "It is kind of royal underwear."

"Still," said Delphie. "I don't want anyone's old underwear! I wanted the money in the Mint!"

All Daisy knew was that she was glad the confession was over. It was a big weight off her shoulders. The Greens could hold their heads up again.

Well, except for Aunt Ivy, who had trespassed into forbidden territory and set off the alarm system. She could still be apprehended for that.

Finally, the waiters collected the remaining dishes, and the guests left the tables and milled about the lawn, where they admired the shrubs, flowers, and sculptures. The president said, "Good-bye and Godspeed," to the Greens, since he would not see them again. Daisy noticed that the small shaving cut on his face had healed.

Aunt Ivy had Mr. James cornered between the water buffalo and the alligator. She was earnestly saying something to him, and he appeared to be struggling to escape. His face was red, and he looked like a trapped fish flapping his fins to get back to his pond, thought Daisy.

All of a sudden, a voice on a loudspeaker flooded the garden.

"Your attention, please! Would Ivy Green please come to the reception hall in the White House. Ivy Green. Report to the reception hall immediately."

Daisy jumped. Aunt Ivy's last name was not Green, but Daisy knew it was her. She was with the Greens, and there was no one else named Ivy here today, she was sure.

The message was repeated three times. It sounded urgent! So the incident in the National Gallery had not been forgotten! No bad deed goes unpunished, Aunt Ivy often told them. Well, it looked like she was right. Aunt Ivy was about to be taken away by the military police.

Daisy hoped her aunt's voice was in good shape, because she was no doubt bound for Sing Sing before the day was over!

CHAPTER 11

Mr. James looked relieved that Aunt Ivy had been summoned elsewhere. He straightened his tie and led her toward the house. Daisy noticed her mother and father following them. They looked worried. It grew quiet in the garden, as the guests stopped their conversations and turned their heads to watch the Greens.

"Let's go see what's up!" said Lois, tugging on Daisy's sleeve.

Daisy had no desire to see her aunt humiliated and sent up the river. But Aunt Ivy was Daisy's own flesh and blood and would need support from her family in a crisis like this.

"It can't be the soup thing," said Lois. "And we know they aren't holding the broken urn against her anymore. It must be breaking and entering at the art gallery!"

"She didn't break and enter!" said Daisy, getting red in the face when she noticed people staring. What if all these guests turned on the Greens for having a criminal element in the family? What if they said her sweet father's animals did not deserve a place in the White House garden now?

"She entered a room that she wasn't supposed to, and that's breaking and entering. It's simple," said Lois.

"Hey, why do they want Aunt Ivy?" shouted Delphie from across the garden.

He ran over and followed the girls, who followed the rest of the Greens.

When they got to the office, Aunt Ivy was saying, "It was just an accident," to the aide in charge.

"Follow me," he said, leading her inside. Mr. James looked like he was relieved to see her go.

The others hung back as Aunt Ivy was led away, but a voice from inside called, "Come in, all of you. I want you all to be here to hear this."

So the deed was so bad they needed witnesses!

It was the president's wife who had called out to them. She was probably trying to soften the blow before the military police came.

"Why would they send for my sister?" murmured Mrs. Green.

"All I know is that it probably isn't to award her a medal," retorted Mr. Green. "She may have caused more disaster at the gallery than we were aware of."

When they all got in the room, the president's wife said, "Please have a seat. We have just had some disturbing news from the National Gallery of Art."

"We were right," whispered Mr. Green. He looked pale. Daisy knew one thing for certain. On the next trip the family took, her father would leave his sister-in-law at home. That is if she ever came home again! It was one thing to cause trouble in a small town. Or in the family. But to cause it on a national scale could be a disaster.

The president's wife went on. "When the guards went in the room to check and found Ivy and Delphie, they noticed a faint smell of gas."

"I didn't do it!" shouted Aunt Ivy.

"Neither did I!" echoed Delphie.

"No, no, of course not!" said the First Lady. "But you see, there was a gas leak in that storeroom that was a serious danger, and it would not have been discovered had it not been for Ivy's entering the room and setting off the alarm!"

It took a while for all this to sink into the

Greens' minds. Was the president's wife saying Aunt Ivy had done something *good*, by breaking and entering?

"If Ivy had not gone into the room, the gas leak would have gone undetected, and eventually there would have been an enormous explosion. It could have injured people in the building and, at the very least, destroyed valuable artwork and equipment."

The Greens all looked shocked. Aunt Ivy was a hero!

"Didn't I tell you?" said Aunt Ivy, shaking her finger. "Didn't I say there was something wrong in that room?"

Daisy had to admit she had said that. Over and over.

"I felt it in my bones, and I have learned to trust my instincts," Aunt Ivy went on. "I don't like to brag, but I have a certain psychic ability, which works well with my skills as a detective. I knew when I came to Washington, I was sent here on a mission, a mission for my government . . ."

The president's wife kept nodding as Aunt Ivy talked. Nodding and smiling. Daisy wanted to stuff a rag in Aunt Ivy's mouth. Didn't she know enough to quit while she was ahead?

"And so," the president's wife interrupted, which was the only way she could talk, "we would like to give you a certificate of merit for saving a national treasure."

Daisy wondered if they had a pile of certificates in a closet somewhere for each time the need arose. How else could they come up with one so fast for Aunt Ivy? It was even in a frame! And it had Aunt Ivy's name on it, Daisy could see, and was signed by the president! This was better than an autograph on a paper napkin. Leave it to Aunt Ivy to come up smelling like a rose! (To quote one of her mother's often-used floral references.)

The First Lady read it out loud: "For meritorious service rendered, the people of this country and the president of the United States award you this certificate of appreciation."

Mr. and Mrs. Green were still speechless, but Aunt Ivy looked as if was the most ordinary thing in the world for her to receive an award from the president. She got up and took it and said thank you, and the aide said she was welcome.

"Call on me anytime," said Aunt Ivy, handing out her cards with her phone number to everyone in the room.

The aide opened the office door, indicating it was time to leave.

"Will wonders never cease!" said Mrs. Green. "It was serendipity. Ivy does something troubling, and it turns into a heroic act."

"I think you owe me an apology," said Aunt Ivy when they got outside. "You don't take my work seriously, you know."

How embarrassing to have to apologize to Aunt Ivy! thought Daisy.

"Come on, Ivy," said Mr. Green. "You know it was just a coincidence that you broke into a room with a gas leak!"

Aunt Ivy shook her head back and forth slowly.

"You just don't get it, do you? It was no coincidence. I was sent here. It was in the stars that my talent be used to save the nation on this trip. I was not here as a tourist, you know."

"I think it's great!" said Delphie. "Wait till I tell the kids at school about this! I might even put it in my report! And wait till Artie and Gladys and Roxanne and Olivia hear about it! Boy, will they be surprised!"

Mr. James was in the hall. He came up to the Greens and said, "I have been assigned to take you to the airport. I'll take you back to the hotel first so you can pack. The plane leaves at five."

On the way to the limo, Aunt Ivy took Mr. James's arm, and Daisy heard her say, "Have you even been to Minnesota? It's a fine place for a summer vacation. If you come when I have time off from the job, I can show you the sights, and maybe you can get a little fishing in. There are ten thousand lakes there, you know . . ."

"Poor Mr. James," said Lois.

"He'll never come," said Daisy.

As her family piled in the limo for the almost-last ride in Washington, Daisy felt good. And if it hadn't been for dear sweet Lois, none of it would have happened. If her friend had not suggested buying lottery tickets, they would still be in Liberty, and all these exciting things would only be a dream. Daisy looked at Lois with admiration. She would have hugged her except it would look funny. She'd have to explain, and it might sound silly.

But the trip had definitely been a success. Even though Aunt Ivy and Delphie had got into a few muddles, it was all straightened out, and there was no longer any need for Daisy to worry.

Her dad had been honored.

The animals were safely installed in their new home.

The Greens had seen Washington.

They had eaten with the president.

And to top it off, Aunt Ivy had been given an award, instead of a jail term!

"Well, I guess all's well that ends well," sighed Mrs. Green.

That appeared to be true. But Daisy wished her sweet mother had not said it so soon. They still were not on that airplane. Anything could happen. And Daisy was very, very superstitious. She didn't like to walk under open ladders or let black cats cross her path. She always knocked on wood. She wished she had some wood to knock on now. Or some salt to throw over her left shoulder.

One of Aunt Ivy's favorite sayings was "He who laughs last laughs best." Daisy always wondered what that meant. But now she thought she knew.

In the airport, Delphie bought some souvenirs. The girls sat down and took their last notes for their school reports.

"This was better than being in school," said Lois, shaking her notebook at Daisy.

"Reports are easy," agreed Daisy.

"I still have half of my notebook empty for the next trip," said Lois.

"What next trip?" demanded Daisy.

The familiar, knowing look came over her friend's face.

"Tell me!" shouted Daisy, shaking Lois by the shoulders.

Lois squinted and appeared to be trying to see something far away.

"I see, I see . . . something like a castle. . . . A big building with guards wearing red suits. Someone is in the window. Who is it?"

Here Lois squinted harder.

"I think it's . . . I think it's Queen Elizabeth!"